My First Phonics Readers BOOK 12

Pop

by Francie Alexander
Illustrated by Maggie Smith

Pop, can I do it?

Pop sits.
I mop and mop.

Can I do it, Pop?

Pop sits and sips.
I dip the pots and pans.

Can I do it?

I sit.

Pop can go to the tip top.

Pop sits.

I sit.

We can do it.